Bush Rescue

DARREL and
SALLY ODGERS

Illustrated by
JANINE DAWSON

To all those Jack Russells, past and present . . .
oh, and to those other dogs, too!
- Darrel and Sally O

To Rosemary & Alan
- Janine Dawson

First American Edition 2016
Kane Miller, A Division of EDC Publishing

Text copyright © Sally and Darrel Odgers 2015
Internal illustrations copyright © Janine Dawson 2015

First published by Scholastic Press a division of Scholastic Australia Pty Limited in 2015.
Cover illustration by Heath McKenzie.

For information contact:
Kane Miller, A Division of EDC Publishing
PO Box 470663
Tulsa, OK 74147-0663
www.kanemiller.com
www.edcpub.com
www.usbornebooksandmore.com

Library of Congress Control Number: 2015954251

Printed and bound in the United States of America

2 3 4 5 6 7 8 9 10

ISBN: 978-1-61067-519-2

Dear Readers,

My name is **Barnaby Station Stamp of Approval,** but you can call me Stamp. My friend Ace and I travel around the country with James Barnaby in a vehicle we call **the Fourby.** I am a **border collie,** so you won't be surprised to learn that I am handsome and clever. Ace is clever too, but James says her second name is Trouble. Ace is not a border collie. She is a mongrel, a dog of mixed breed.

This is our second big Pup Patrol adventure. James and I had visited Cousin Jeannie and met Ace there. Ace started traveling with us, but we didn't know her very well yet. We were driving towards a town called Jasper when we smelled the smoke . . .

Yours,
Stamp
Pup Patroller

Who's Who.

The Crew of the Fourby

James Barnaby. James is 19. He wants to be a vet.

Barnaby Station Stamp of Approval. Me. A clever, handsome border collie.

Ace. A dog of mixed breed and bad manners.

Other Family and Friends

Dad and Mum Barnaby. James's parents back at Barnaby Station.

Dr. Jeannie and Trump. James's cousin (a vet) and her Jack Russell terrier.

Rusty. An old border collie we know.

In Jasper

Daisy Ado. A Major Mitchell cockatoo.

Doc Jensen. The vet in Jasper.

Mink. A Siamese cat.

Bob Dean. An old man.

Hector. Bob's dog.

Tina. Bob's granddaughter.

Stamp's Glossary

Barnaby Station Stamp of Approval.
Pedigreed animals often have long names.
My parents are named Barnaby Station Penny
Black and Brightwood Superlative.
Border collies. Herding dogs that came from
the Anglo-Scottish borders. They are one of the
most intelligent dogs in the world.
The Fourby. Four-wheel drive SUV.

Chapter One

Smoke

The old house was dark and full of smoke. Although James had a flashlight, I couldn't see much and I couldn't follow my nose. I sniffed at the floor and sneezed. I stopped and pawed at my snout.

James sneezed, too. The smoke made his eyes stream with tears. He mopped at them with a big handkerchief. "This is no good," he wheezed. He lifted the handkerchief again, then yelled, "Ouch!"

"Ace, what did you do?" I asked between sneezes.

"Gahrr-ng-ng-ng," said Ace. That was what it sounded like, anyway.

"Give it back," said James. Through the smoke, I saw him bend and pull at something in Ace's jaws. "Drop it!" he said. "Now!"

"Ace, stop that," I growled.

Ace opened her jaws and gave me a

cranky look.

"What?" she said, then spat out a bit of fabric. She had grabbed James's handkerchief and tried to swallow it.

James blew his nose. "Let's go," he said. "Someone else must have let the old dog out."

Just then, we heard a **pawful** coughing sound coming from the smoke.

So, why were James, Ace and I in a dark house full of smoke, looking for a dog that wasn't there? It was because James wanted to help Tina . . . but that's not the beginning of the story.

It started one morning when we stopped at a post office so James could collect a package from home.

We'd been driving for a while and it was

hot. Of course, James had the windows rolled down to let in some fresh air, but I was tired of sitting still. I am a border collie, after all. I need plenty of exercise. I was also tired of Ace.

I sat in my harness on the passenger seat. Ace was in a **pet carrier** on the backseat. She spent the whole morning complaining. Sometimes she yapped, "Let me out! Let me out!" over and over. Sometimes she scraped the door of the carrier with her front paws. Her claws went, *Scritchhhh-scritchhhhhh! Scritchhhh-scritchhhhhh!* The worst thing, though, was when she whined.

All dogs whine sometimes. We do it when we're nervous, or excited. Ace's whine is so high-pitched. It was like a mosquito zinging away behind me. It made my teeth tingle and my ears feel

funny. I kept shaking my head.

"Stop that!" I told her every so often.

"Eeeeee . . ." went Ace through her
nose.

When James parked the Fourby next
to the little post office, Ace stopped. "I'm
thirsty," she said.

I wasn't surprised.

James got out of the Fourby and

unclipped my harness from the seat. "Coming, Stamp?"

I sprang out, stretched and shook myself.

James poured some water into my bowl. I lapped it up and then sniffed the air. I always love to sniff the air in a new place.

Ace started yapping and scrabbling in her carrier. "Let me out! Let me out!"

James sighed and opened the carrier door. Ace shot out like a cork from a bottle. James grabbed her and clipped on a leash. "Sit, Ace," he said.

Ace paid no attention.

"Sit, Ace." James sounded patient.

Ace snorted. Then she darted to my water bowl and lapped noisily. She snarled at me when I tried to keep drinking.

"Ace!" James tugged the leash.

Ace squatted and made a **puddle**. Then she looked up at James. "Treat?"

"You have to be obedient to get a treat," I said. "Watch and learn." I sat down and folded my tail neatly around me. I lifted one paw and cocked my head.

Ace got on her hind legs and danced around. "Treat! Treat! Treat!" she yapped.

James took a **Tidge-Treat** from his pocket. "Good boy, Stamp!" He held it out to me.

I reached out to accept it **pawlitely**. Ace snatched it out of James's hand.

She backed off, crunching. "*That's* how you get a treat," she said.

"Oh Ace, you're trouble!" laughed James. He picked Ace up and held her under one arm while he gave me a treat. Then he rubbed her ears. "It's not her

fault," he said to me. "She was never taught any manners when she was a pup. She'll soon learn to behave."

I hoped he was right.

Stamp's Glossary

Pawful. Awful, for dogs.

Pawlitely. Politely, for dogs.

Pet carrier. A cage that keeps small dogs and cats safe in cars or on trips to the vet.

Puddle. Dogs don't have bathrooms like humans do. They have the ground. Best not to jump in these puddles, though.

Tidge-Treats. Crunchy delicious treats made in Doggeroo. My friend Rusty loves them.

Chapter Two
The Radio

James left us tied under a big pepper tree while he walked into the post office. After a few minutes, he came out carrying a package. He put it on the Fourby's hood and undid it. Inside was a **radio**. James looked pleased. "Now we can call Barnaby Station from anywhere in the country. Even when there's no mobile phone signal!"

I watched as James set up the radio.

Ace chased bugs in the grass and yapped at **rainbow lorikeets**. I saw heat shimmering over the road.

James had no trouble mounting the antenna to the Fourby and setting up the **HF** radio beside the **CB radio.** "All set. Let's give Dad a call!" He took the microphone, listened and said, "This is **VK7NJT. Over**." He said that a few more times and listened patiently.

Ace pricked up her ears. "What's he doing?"

"He's using the radio," I said. I had learned about this back home at Barnaby Station. "It lets James talk to Dad Barnaby and to anyone else who has one."

"VK7NJT . . . this is VK7OK," said a voice. "Good morning, James!"

It was Dad Barnaby! I wagged my tail and barked twice.

Dad Barnaby laughed. "Hello, Stamp! I see you've picked up the radio, James. Over."

"We're just at the post office now, Dad. Over."

"Great," said Dad Barnaby. "Did you get to see Jeannie? Over."

"We saw Jeannie," said James. "She's great. We got a pup from her for Pepper Plains Farm. Anyway, better go now, Dad.

We're heading to Jasper for some lunch. Over."

"Take care, son," said Dad Barnaby. "I heard there are bushfires out that way. Over."

"Okay," said James. "Say hi to Mum. This is VK7NJT clearing the frequency."

"Bye, James. VK7OK also clear."

James puffed out his cheeks as he hung up the microphone. "Phew! I thought Jeannie might have told him about Ace." He looked hard at Ace, who was scratching her ear. "I don't want to tell Dad and Mum about you until you have learned some manners," he told her.

Ace **smarled**.

James opened the Fourby door and I jumped back into my seat. Ace didn't want to go back in the pet carrier. She growled and scrabbled and stuck her paws out so James couldn't fit her through the door. "All right!" he said. "But you have to behave!" He tied her leash firmly so she couldn't jump off the seat.

And off we went.

I looked back between the seats. Ace had her nose poked out the window. Her ears blew back in the wind.

After a while, James frowned. "That sky doesn't look good," he said to me.

I looked out the window. There was a heavy cloud out there, and it didn't look right. I sniffed the air. No wonder the cloud looked wrong. It was smoke!

"That'll be the bushfire Dad mentioned. Looks like it's pretty close to Jasper. We'd better head somewhere else for lunch."

The cloud grew heavier and the smell

of smoke grew stronger. Flakes of ash landed on the Fourby's windshield and came in through the windows.

Ace sneezed.

"Better wind those windows up, eh Stamp?" said James. Just then, I heard a whoosh and a scream and a flapping noise behind us. Ace started shrieking and scrabbling.

"What the—?" said James, raising his voice over the noise.

Then something really strange happened. Someone said, "Oopsy daisy!" from the backseat.

Stamp's Glossary

CB radio. Citizens' band radio.

HF. High frequency.

Over. This is what radio operators say to let the other person know it is their turn to talk.

Radio. James's radio is not the kind that plays music. It's the kind people use to talk to one another.

Rainbow lorikeets. Noisy brightly colored birds.

Smarl. A dog grin. Some dogs smarl a lot. Some don't do it at all.

VK7NJT. This is a call sign. It is a bit like a phone number but used for radios.

Chapter Three

Daisy Ado

James and I turned around in a hurry. Ace yapped and fought her leash, but we weren't looking at her. We were staring at someone else who was flapping and yelling, "Oopsy daisy!"

"It's a **Major Mitchell** cockatoo!" said James. "Ace, stop that!"

"Out! Out! Out!" yapped Ace. She snapped at the bird and it fluttered onto the back of the seat. It stuck its stripy

crest up, half opened its wings and screamed back at Ace.

James got out of the Fourby and opened the back door. "Ace, behave!" He unclipped Ace from the seat and bundled her over beside me.

Then he stood staring at the cockatoo. It hunched its wings and screeched again.

"Who are you?" asked James.

"Daisy, Daisy Ado," said the cockatoo.

"You're called Daisy?" said James. "Daisy A-doo?"

"Daisy, Daisy Ado," said the bird again. It used human talk. Some cockatoos and parrots can do that.

James laughed. "Daisy Ado! I suppose that means you make a lot of fuss and **ado** about things?"

I wagged my tail and Ace tried to scramble back over the seat to get at Daisy.

"What are you doing in our Fourby?" I asked the cockatoo.

She cocked her head. "I had to land somewhere!" She let her striped crest fall back flat. "You talk?"

"I'm a border collie," I explained. "I'm a **herding dog**. I need to be able to communicate with different animals and birds to do my job. My name is Barnaby Station Stamp of Approval, but you can call me Stamp."

"My name is Daisy Ado. You can call me Daisy Ado. Who is the horrible hairy one?" Daisy made a pecking movement towards Ace who was still carrying on. "If you don't stop that, I shall peck you," she said. "And remember—I can crack nuts with this beak!"

Ace stopped yapping.

"That's Ace," I said. "She's not horrible. She just has no manners."

"Hmm," said Daisy. She shuffled her wings and preened a few feathers back into place. "I had to land somewhere," she said again. "I'm not used to all this flying."

"Why were you flying, then?" I asked. I'd worked out that she was a pet cockatoo, not a wild one. Wild cockatoos don't use human speech and they're afraid of dogs. Daisy wasn't afraid of me. She had even put Ace in her place!

"I escaped the fire," said Daisy. She settled more comfortably on the back of the seat, digging her claws into the leather. "It was awful."

James stood back from the open Fourby door. "Out you go, Daisy Ado," he said. "Fly off home."

Daisy shuffled her wings again. "You have got to be joking," she said, and tucked one claw up under her chest feathers.

"Go!" said James, clapping his hands. "Shoo!"

Daisy yawned.

James reached in and put his arm in front of her. Then he nudged her tail with his other hand. Daisy stepped onto his wrist, but when he tried to lift her out of the Fourby, she jumped off and settled back onto the seat.

"Well!" said James. "We'll have to go into Jasper and find your owner."

Daisy opened one beady eye. "I live with Al," she said to me, and closed it again.

Stamp's Glossary

Ado. A big fuss. Say it like this: A-doo.

Cockatoo. A bird of the parrot family. Cockatoos all have crests.

Crest. Long feathers on top of a cockatoo's head. They can lift them up and down.

Herding dog. A dog bred to look after sheep or cattle.

Major Mitchell. A type of cockatoo with a pink head and wings and a red, yellow and white crest. Sometimes called a Leadbeater's cockatoo.

Chapter Four

Doc Jensen

James tried to put Daisy Ado in the pet carrier, but she edged away across the backseat and hissed at him. "Oh, all right!" He gave up. "I suppose you must be used to being in a vehicle or you wouldn't have flown in."

"I am," Daisy told me. She shot a nasty look at Ace. "But not with yappy, snappy, scrappy dogs."

James drove on towards Jasper.

As we got closer to town, we came to a roadblock. A firefighter held up her hand for James to stop.

"What's your business in Jasper?" she asked. She nodded to the **license plate** on the Fourby. "I see you're not a local."

"We were going to detour," said James, "but then this Major Mitchell flew in through the window." He pointed into the backseat. "It must be someone's pet."

"I see," said the firefighter. "We have fires out of control. We've saved the town, but it was touch and go. We're still on **red alert**, in case the **wind changes** again. Everything is a mess. Most of the fire squad has gone to outlying farms that are still under threat." She frowned. "It's dangerous. We don't need sightseers."

"We'll leave as soon as I get this cocky back to her owners," said James. "Do you know who she belongs to?"

She shook her head. "Look—um—"

"I'm James," said James. "This is Stamp and Ace." He pointed to us. "We definitely don't want to get in anyone's way."

The firefighter considered. "Doc Jensen might know who the cocky belongs to. He runs the vet clinic on the edge of town. He's really busy, though. His assistants are away fighting fires."

"Could he use some help?" asked
James. "I'm planning to be a vet and
Stamp is useful with cattle and sheep."

"In that case," said the firefighter, "just
drive on down the road and turn left into
Russell Road. Doc's place is on the right."

She waved us past the roadblock and
James drove on. The smoke grew heavier,

so James switched on the headlights.

The Fourby swung to the left and we drove on very slowly. "I think this must be it," he said. "I'll be back in a tick." He started to get out of the Fourby, then turned back. "Ace, please leave that bird alone."

Ace sat down and looked good. James

thought he was training her. I knew it was really what Daisy had said about being able to crack nuts with her beak. Ace's nose was smaller than a nut.

When James had gone, I put my paws on the dashboard and peered out through the murk. I turned my nose to the gap James had left in the window and sniffed. I detected the sour smell of burned ground and wet charcoal. It made me sneeze.

"What are you doing?" asked Ace. It was the first thing she'd said since Daisy threatened to peck her.

"I'm finding my bearings," I said. "If James wants to help out, we might be here for a while." I turned to Daisy. "Do you know this place?"

"No," she said.

"Isn't it the vet's place?" I asked.

"How should I know?" Daisy raised her crest. "I've never been to the vet. I am a healthy bird. I have plenty of food and water and a fine aviary—well, I did, until a tree fell across it. I was lucky to escape with all my feathers!"

I looked back out the window. The vet clinic had two sprawling buildings with a garden and a lot of runs and cages built out to the side. One wall of the bigger building was blackened and the window was smashed. Some of the shrubs in the yard were burned and the wooden gates looked charred. Everything that wasn't burned looked wet and soggy. No wonder it smelled bad.

James came back with a man in a white coat smudged with soot. He pointed to Daisy, but the man shook his head.

James looked disappointed. "Mr. Jensen—"

"Call me Doc," said the man.

"Doc. Do you have anywhere Daisy can stay while we try to find her owner?"

"She can go in a cage," said Doc. "Do you need to crate your dogs?"

"No, they'll be fine with me," said James. "At least, Stamp will. Ace is a bit tricky, but she's improving."

Doc sighed. "Bring your things into the cottage. Then I'll put you to work. You sure about this? It will be a long day and probably a long night."

James nodded. "Glad to help. I'm trying to get experience in all kinds of situations before I start my vet training next year."

James pulled his sleeping bag and our blankets out of the back of the Fourby.

Daisy hopped onto James's shoulder and Doc led us around the back.

The cottage was a plain little house. It smelled of smoke, but the fire hadn't damaged it. "My student helpers sleep here sometimes," said Doc, "but they're out with the Rural Fire Brigade now."

James dumped his gear in the kitchen. Daisy hopped off his shoulder and went to roost on the back of a chair.

"Leave her there for now," said Doc. "Majors aren't usually destructive and she seems very tame." He took a plate of sandwiches out of the fridge and offered them to James. "Grab some of these and I'll put you to work."

He went off and left the four of us in the cottage.

Stamp's Glossary

License plate. The license plates on a vehicle show which state it comes from.
Red alert. This happens when everyone has to be ready to act during an emergency.
Wind change. Wind makes bushfires move along and get bigger and unpredictable.

Chapter Five

Working for Doc

"What can we do first?" asked James. We were in the clinic with Doc after lunch.

"The fire went through Jasper in the night," Doc explained. "Most of the town survived, but it was a close call and people who are not fighting other fires are watching for **spot fires** around town. Some people lost trees, sheds and fences, and at one point we thought we'd all have to **evacuate** to Corella, down the highway. A lot of folk whose houses were damaged are at the **evacuation center** down at the town hall."

James nodded again.

"Most people in Jasper have pets or livestock," Doc continued. "If it's just one dog, it's not so bad. It stays with the family. But sometimes it's chickens or ducks, or two or three cats. Then there are the ponies and pet lambs and goats and house cows. Understand?"

"Yes," said James. "There isn't room for all of those in a car or the town hall."

"A lot of the cats panicked and ran. Last night, when we thought we'd lose the town, people let animals out of cages or runs and hoped they'd get clear," said Doc. "Now there are animals wandering everywhere . . . It's dangerous for them."

"We can help find them," said James.

"We?" asked Doc.

"Stamp knows how to herd up sheep and cattle, even ducks and chickens," said James. "He's smart. His parents are champion **trial dogs**."

"Excellent," said Doc. "Okay, you go after any straying animals. See if you can find out where they came from if they don't have collars. If no one knows, bring them back here and put them in the runs or cages or stables. Don't worry about the owners at this stage. The main thing is to get those animals off the streets and away from any damaged buildings or spot fires."

"We'll start now," said James.

"Thanks." Doc handed James a large round badge. "This is what my students wear. If people see it they'll know you're working with me. Grab a couple of leashes and halters . . . cages too . . . oh, and some treats and heavy gloves."

"I have Tidge-Treats and the gloves I use for **fencing** in the Fourby," said James. "We have a pet carrier too."

Someone banged on the door and James opened it. A woman with a cat basket rushed in. "Doc! We found Lilly! She's lost a lot of fur, but I think she's okay . . ."

"Come on, dogs," said James. He grabbed a handful of ropes and leashes from a peg by the door and we followed him out.

We piled back into the Fourby. James started whistling, cheerfully.

"What's he doing that for?" asked Ace, shaking her ears.

"James loves a challenge," I told her. "He was going to do the sensible thing and stay away from the bushfire area, but now that we're here, he's all set for adventure."

"What if I don't want an adventure?" grumbled Ace.

"You can get back in the pet carrier," I said, and Ace gave me a nasty look.

James started the Fourby and we drove slowly along Russell Road, heading farther into town.

The trees and grass on one side of the road were burned and the bitter smell made me sneeze again. There was a fence set back from the road. The wooden posts were black and some were burned through, letting the wires sag and tangle. Patches of black ground still smoked. Then I noticed a lamb trying to get through the wires.

"Stand!" I barked.

James saw the lamb and stopped. He let me out. "Go see," he told me.

The lamb stared as I trotted towards it. Its wool was gray with smoke and charcoal.

I stared back at the lamb. I have a strong **eye**. "It's all right," I said. "I'm here to help."

"*Ba-a-adddd*," it bleated.

Sheep always tell you when they're in trouble.

"Where your **flock**?" I asked.

"What flock?" said the lamb. Then it looked at James, who had gotten out of the Fourby. "He not Barry."

"No, he James. You live with other sheep?" I asked.

"*Baa-aa-rry*!" bleated the lamb.

I realized this was a pet lamb. I couldn't explain that to James, so I told the lamb what to do. "Run to James. Show happy."

"*Baa-aa-rry*!"

"James kind. James friend. Show happy."

The lamb trotted up to James and butted at his legs.

"Hello there." James rubbed it behind its ears. He looked up and down the road. "I'm guessing you're a pet? No collar, though." He lifted the lamb into the back of the Fourby. Ace started yapping.

"She silly," said the lamb. Ace looked insulted and stopped yapping.

Down the road a bit, we found two cows and a mob of eleven sheep.

"Can't put them in the Fourby," said James. "The paddock on the other side is empty, though."

He opened the gate and stood back. "Okay, Stamp. In with them."

I wagged my tail to say I understood. This was the kind of job we had practiced back home at Barnaby Station. I watched my mother and father do it when I was just a puppy.

I trotted around the animals, bringing them into a mob. "All safe," I told them. When I had them collected, I guided them to the gate. One old ewe turned and tried to stare me down. I stared back and gave her the eye. She dipped her head.

"I butt," she warned.

"I nip," I said.

"I stamp," she added, stamping her front hoof.

"No, *I'm* Stamp," I said. I gave a little bark and rushed at her. She wheeled and trotted after the others.

James closed the gate behind them. "Good boy, Stamp."

I wagged my tail and pretended that I couldn't hear Ace's **snigger** from the Fourby.

Stamp's Glossary

Evacuate. Leave home for safety.

Evacuation center. A safe building where people can stay while their homes are in danger.

Eye. Herding dogs like me can command sheep with our stare.

Fencing. Making or mending fences.

Flock. Group of sheep.

Snigger. To laugh in a naughty way. Only dogs and people with bad manners snigger.

Spot fires. Fires that start from flying embers or burning twigs.

Trial dogs. Dogs that enter sheep dog trials, which are competitions.

Chapter Six
Mink

By evening, we had picked up another
pet lamb and a wandering goat and taken
them back to Doc's place. They were all
tired and thirsty.

Then James had a new idea. He asked
Doc for a whiteboard and set it up at
the clinic gate. Then he wrote a list of
the animals we had found and where
they were. He and Doc updated the list
as owners came searching for their pets

and livestock. Other people brought in straying dogs and cats. Then, as we drove around for a last check before it got too dark, someone flagged down the Fourby and handed James a goose.

"It was in my garden eating grass," the man explained.

"What's that thing?" Ace demanded.

"It's a goose," I said as James took the goose and tucked it into the pet carrier.

The goose hissed and honked and Ace snarled back. "Out! Out! Mine!"

"Don't be silly," I said. "You don't even *like* the carrier."

"I don't like this," she said. "It's too crowded." She grumbled, showing her sharp little fangs.

"It's only one goose," I pointed out.

"One goose *is* too many," said a Siamese cat. We'd found her yowling on a street corner. She had a collar with an address, but when we went to look, the house was half burned and there was no one there.

"My people went without me," said the cat, who said her name was Mink. She licked her paw and swiped it behind her ear. "I was up a tree. Then a big truck came and shot water all over the place. I had to run or I would have been drenched. I was afraid. I hate water." She sounded calm, but I saw she was twitching now and then. She turned to Ace, who was still snarling at the goose. "What's your story, dog? Did your house burn down?"

"None of your business," snapped Ace.

"Did she run away from the fires like me?" Mink asked me. She edged forward to sniff at Ace. Ace snapped, just missing Mink's nose.

"Stop it, Ace," I growled. She was being extra grumpy today! I turned to Mink. "James and I adopted Ace a few days ago. Her first people didn't look after her so she needed a new home. She doesn't have good manners yet."

"She's yours, then? Not an **evacuee**?" said Mink. She sounded surprised.

"Of course she's ours!" I said. Then I explained how we first met Ace. "We were choosing a dog **apprentice** for my friend, old Rusty. We met Ace at the same time. James and I chose her to come with us."

Ace glared at me.

Suddenly, I understood why she was being so grumpy about the goose and Mink and even the lambs and goat. "Ace," I said, "did you think James and I were going to *adopt* all these evacuees?"

"Aren't you?" grumbled Ace. "Why wouldn't you get this cat and this goose and that lamb? The cat has *manners*."

"We *chose* you," I said. "Mink and the goose and these others have their own homes. They'll go back home to their people when the fires are out and everything is cleared up."

"Oh," said Ace. She stopped glaring at me and licked her nose nervously.

"You're *ours*," I said. "And we're *yours*. You're staying with us, wherever we go."

Mink sniffed. "Just as well," she said. "I can't imagine anyone else—" She broke off as James stopped the Fourby outside a big hall. There were vehicles parked all around and a lot of older people and children around.

"Jasper Town Hall," said James looking at a big sign. "This must be the evacuation center Doc told us about." James got out and went to talk to a tall woman with a **megaphone** and a clipboard. He showed her a piece of paper. The woman nodded, then started talking through the megaphone. Her voice boomed so loudly we could hear it in the Fourby.

"Attention! James is helping Doc Jensen with straying pets and livestock. He has a list of those found so far. If any of these is yours, please let him know."

She read off James's list. "Two pet
lambs, two Jersey cows, eleven ewes,
one goose. One **Saanen** nanny goat. A
Siamese cat called Mink. Three terrier
mixes, one red heeler, a beagle, two tabby
cats and one black tom."

Five people started moving towards
James right away.

"That's one of my people!" purred Mink as a girl ran towards the Fourby.

"Mink!" The girl put her hand against the window and Mink moved to rub her face against the glass. "We were so worried when we had to leave without you. I'm so glad you're safe!"

There was a lot of coming and going after that. The girl told James that Mink was used to going for walks on a leash and so she could stay at the hall for now. James handed her over, smiling.

An old man claimed the goose, but said there was nowhere to keep her.

"My house just needs a good clean and some drying out," he said. "We can move back in in a few days, as long as the wind doesn't change and bring the fires back. Until then . . ."

"Doc has boarding pens," said James.

The old man nodded gratefully.

"By the way," said James. He borrowed the megaphone and started booming out, "We found a Major Mitchell cockatoo along the highway. I think its name is Daisy Ado. Does Daisy belong to anyone here?"

No one answered. The old man with the goose said his neighbor had a galah named Danny.

"That's here in its carry cage," said the organizer.

James shrugged. "Well, if anyone can think of who she could belong to, she's at Doc Jensen's place, in the cottage." He took a deep breath. "Is anyone missing any animals? Give me descriptions and your names and what you want me to do if I find them. I'll see what we can manage tomorrow when it's light."

After that, of course, quite a few people crowded around saying their dogs or cats had run away in the night, or they'd let their ducks or hens out and hadn't seen them since. One girl said her donkey bolted when a gum tree exploded behind its stable.

James scribbled down names and information. I yawned and settled for a nap. I was just drowsing off when Ace

got up on her hind legs and peered at me between the seats. "Stamp?"

I rolled my eyes up without lifting my head. "Ace?"

"Are all these others going home?"

I yawned again. "Yes. Sooner or later."

"But I'm staying with you and James?"

"Yes, of course," I said. Then I really did go to sleep.

Stamp's Glossary

Apprentice. A younger dog or person learning the job from someone more experienced.

Evacuees. People or animals who have left their homes for safety.

Megaphone. A mouthpiece that lets people speak really loudly.

Saanen. A white goat breed from Switzerland.

Chapter Seven
Wind Change

Back at Doc Jensen's place, James helped
feed and check all the animals we'd
rescued. Then we went to the cottage
to sleep. Daisy, like most parrots and
cockatoos, had gone to **roost** as soon as it
was dark. She ruffled her wings and hissed
sleepily when we came in. When she saw
it was us, she tucked up one claw and
settled again.

James fed us kibble and got into his

sleeping bag. I lay down beside him and Ace crept up under his arm and licked his chin.

James spluttered and patted her. "Okay, Ace. Go to sleep."

Ace sighed and put her paw on James's arm. "Mine," she said. She sounded happy.

I sighed, too. I *wanted* Ace to be happy. A happy dog is a good dog, mostly. Happy dogs are nice to be around. I didn't want her to get any wrong ideas, though.

"James is *ours*," I said firmly.

Ace sat up. "Mine! Mine!"

"Ours!" I said.

Ace growled.

Daisy popped open her beady eyes and hissed. "Be quiet. I warned you—I can crack nuts with this beak," she said. "Walnuts. Brazil nuts, even!"

I think she was lying, but Ace stopped growling, sighed and went to sleep.

I woke up suddenly. The wind was gusting and roaring outside the cottage and I heard a siren *hee-hawing* in the distance. I sat up and sneezed. We'd become used to the bitter smell of smoke and burned wood, but there was fresh smoke in the air.

This felt dangerous, so I pawed at James's hand and barked.

"What is it, Stamp?" He sounded sleepy. I jumped up and trotted to the cottage door. I jammed my nose against the gap and sniffed hard. I barked again.

Daisy squawked and Ace jumped up with a yelp.

James wriggled out of his sleeping bag. "That sounds bad," he said. I didn't think he meant the noise Ace was making.

He opened the door and we looked out. The sky was lit by a dull red glow and there was too much smoke to see. Embers blew in on the wind.

"Ouch!" said James, slapping at his arm.

By now, other animals were awake and frightened. I heard lambs bleating from one of the pens and three cats **caterwauling**. The red heeler barked, the terriers yipped and the beagle howled.

Ace surprised me by tossing back her head and howling, too. My **hackles** prickled and I wanted to join in. I turned to James. He would know what to do.

"Wait here," said James. He pulled on a jacket and left the cottage. I thought I

heard him banging on a door somewhere
in the distance.

Very soon after that, I heard voices.
James was coming back with Doc.

"Spot fires," Doc was saying. "And
one big flare-up at the other end of town.
The wind changed. I called the center
and more people are coming in. Some are

bringing animals here now."

"Do you need me to go back to the center?" asked James.

"No, I'll go," said Doc. "You stay here. I'll send people here, so if you can direct them to whatever pens are empty, that'll be a help. If any bad injuries come in . . ." He frowned. "The phones are down."

"But then how did you call the center?" asked James.

Doc grinned. "CB," he said. "One of the blokes directing at the center is a **trucker** so I called his rig."

"I have a radio in the Fourby," said James.

"Excellent," said Doc. "If you need me, give me a call."

"Okay."

"If the worst comes to it, turn on the sprinklers," said Doc. "If it's worse than that, let out what you can and *go*."

Then he was gone.

James drew in a deep breath. Then he clicked his fingers to me. "Ace, stay here," he said. "Leave the bird alone." He checked that Daisy was out of Ace's reach. Then he picked Ace up and gave her a hug. We both went out.

James drove the Fourby as close to the cottage as he could. Then we went around checking on the animals. They were all afraid. Well, I was afraid too. It's natural for animals to be scared of fire.

Another fire truck tore along the road with its siren blaring. Very soon, we saw lights coming from the other direction. It turned out to be a woman in a van. She had eight cats in cages.

"Eight!" said James.

"I'm from Just-Purr Cattery," said

the woman. "The fire's closing in behind us and we were told to leave. We got the cats out and someone said Doc had room for them. My partner's still there helping out." She bit her lip. "I can stay to look after the cats."

"Fine," said James. "You'll have to put the cages wherever there's space for them. We're close to full up."

The woman started unloading cat cages. They were very big, so James helped her until two men arrived with a cow and a calf in a trailer.

The cow didn't want to come down the ramp, but I herded her into one of the last pens. One of the owners brought the calf. A minute later, a man on a motorbike brought a large spotted rabbit.

James stared at it. "I think that's one of the pets on my list!" He pulled the list out of his jacket pocket. "Yes . . . white rabbit with black spots and a moustache-shaped patch. This is Humpty Bun."

The man shrugged. "Yeah, I figured it was a pet."

"The owner will be relieved." James sighed. "But I have no idea where to put him. He can't go in with cats or dogs." He thought about it. "I know!" He took Humpty Bun from the biker and took it into the cottage. He put the rabbit in the bathroom and closed the door.

After that, there was a lull and James and I went back to the front yard. The red glow in the sky was still there and now there was a bright splash of orange up the road. "Spot fire," said James.

"We'll see to that," said one of the men who had brought the cow. "We have wet sacks in the trailer." They drove back up the road and soon the spot fire was out.

The embers were still flying, so James turned on all the sprinklers. There were even some on the roof.

We heard a clatter of hooves on the road and a pony trotted up to the gate. A girl about James's age slid down. "Is Doc here?" she asked. She sounded worried, but she took the time to pat me.

She smelled good, of hay, horse and biscuits. I gave her my **stamp of approval** right away.

"Doc's at the evacuation center at the hall," said James.

"Oh . . ." She frowned. "Who are you?"

"I'm James Barnaby," said James. "We were just passing when a Major Mitchell flew in the Fourby window. It wouldn't

get out, so we brought it here to see if we could find the owner. Its name's Daisy Ado . . . I think."

The girl stared at James. "I have no idea what you're talking about. What are you doing *here*?"

"I'm helping Doc," said James. "I suppose you want to put your pony in with the pet lambs? It can't go in the cottage. And Humpty Bun's in the bathroom."

"Whoa!" said the girl. "Humpty Bun?"

"A rabbit."

"Right. No, I don't want to leave my pony here. I came to see if Doc had seen my grandad . . . Bob Dean." She frowned. "He lives over near the cattery with his old dog, Hector. Mum was on her way to get him, but our truck got a flat. Someone else offered to take him to the evacuation center, but now Grandad's disappeared."

"He's not here," said James.

"Grandad called Mum to say Hector had been left behind. Then he said he was coming here because he'd heard straying animals were being brought to Doc's. Then the phones went down."

"I'll call Doc on the radio," said James. In a minute, he was talking to Doc Jensen the way he talked to Dad Barnaby.

When he finished, he came back to the girl. "Doc says your grandad's not at the evacuation center anymore. He said he was going to his daughter's place."

The girl looked really worried now. "Stubborn old coot! I bet he's trying to get someone to take him back home to look for Hector."

"Wait here," said James. "If your grandad shows up, tell him to stay put and that I've gone to look for Hector."

71

"You can't do that," said the girl. "The old dog's deaf and half blind. He won't come to you."

"Stamp will find him," said James. "I'll take Ace, too. She always barks at strange dogs, so she'll let me know if there's one around."

The girl shook her head slowly. "I still have no idea what you're talking about. But Grandad's place is two doors from the cattery. It's on Stoat Street."

"We saw that street earlier," said James. "Now you wait here—um . . . ?"

"Tina," said the girl.

"Tina. Your pony can go in with the cows if it's not for long. If anyone else shows up with animals, please tell them we're nearly full up . . . but rabbits can go in the bathroom."

Stamp's Glossary

Caterwauling. Making a loud terrible noise, as cats do.

Hackles. Hair on the back of a dog's neck that stands up when we're angry or excited.

Roost. When birds settle for the night in a tree or a perch.

Stamp of approval. An award of honor. Only I can give it.

Trucker. Someone whose job is to drive trucks.

Chapter Eight

Finding Hector

James fetched Ace from the cottage. Then we all got in the Fourby and drove towards the dull red glow in the sky. It was much duller by now, and as we came nearer, the smoke seemed heavier and wetter, as if some of it was steam.

The fire truck was up near the cattery and water splashed everywhere. James pulled up the Fourby outside an old house  two doors down. The paint looked blistered and a window had broken. James got us out and put Ace on a leash. Then we walked around the yard. There was a kennel in the garden with a blanket and empty bowl. James whistled.

Ace shook her head. "What's he doing now?" she asked.

"Calling a dog called Hector," I said. "He probably won't hear though. If you smell a dog, or hear one, yap."

"You always tell me *not* to yap," grumbled Ace.

"You can yap when you need to yap. Just don't yap for no reason. Remember— James is *ours*. He'll never let us down. We have to help him."

Ace sniffed the ground. "There's been a dog here, but he's not here now," she said. "Do I yap now?"

"No."

James gave up on the garden and knocked on the door. It swung open, so we stepped in. "Hector?" called James.

The old house was dark and full of smoke and when James tried to turn on

a light, nothing happened. James and
I started sneezing. James got out his
handkerchief. That's when Ace decided
she needed to eat the handkerchief. Why?
I don't know . . .

"Gahrr-ng-ng-ng . . ."

James told her to drop it and they had
a little tug-of-war. I was distracted by
the fuss and it wasn't until James decided
we were wasting our time that we heard
a pawful coughing sound. Straight after
that, I caught my first real whiff of dog.

I trotted away and pawed at the
nearest door. Then I sniffed hard under
the gap . . . and sneezed.

Ace came up beside me and sniffed
as well. Then she got up on her hind
legs and jumped around, coughing and
yapping and battering at the door. "Dog!
Old dog! Man! Old man!"

"Okay, okay!" James stumbled up behind us. He was breathing through the handkerchief Ace had tried to swallow. He opened the door. It stuck, then popped open and a gush of steam hit us all in the face.

An old man was sitting on the floor with his back against a bathtub. It was full of water. He had his arm around a very old dog. He was a black Labrador whose muzzle and eyebrows were all gray. The old man had a towel tied over his mouth. He looked at us and mumbled, "Shut the door! There's a fire out there."

James shut the door. "Mr. Dean? And Hector?"

"Bob Dean, that's me. I bet that granddaughter of mine sent you after me," he said, pushing the towel down. "We're okay in here. See? I have wet

towels. I filled the tub."

"The fire's nearly out," said James. "If you like, I can take you and Hector to the evacuation center, or your daughter's place or . . . wherever else you want to go."

Bob Dean thought about that. Then he looked at me. "Nice dog you got there. Real handsome. I always liked borders, though my Hector's a Lab. And what's that?" He pointed at Ace. "A tracker rat?"

"Ace is a terrier mix," said James, raising his voice over the noise Ace was still making. "She always barks at strange dogs."

"No point her barking at Hector," said the old man. "He's stone deaf."

Ace must have heard him, because she piped down. Then she strutted up to the old dog and sat down in front of him. She reached up to lick his nose. The old dog beat his tail gently.

Ace curled her little whip of a tail around and lifted her front paw. "Treat?" she said.

James laughed, sneezed and gave her a treat. Then he gave one to me and one to old Hector as well. After that, he helped Bob Dean stand up. He picked up Hector and carried him slowly back through the smoky house and out the door.

Bob Dean stopped to look over towards the cattery. "That's a mess," he said. Then he looked up. "Wind's dropped. I guess they'll soon have this all under control."

Chapter Nine

On The Road Again

Soon we were back at Doc's place. The wind had dropped and the sun was coming up.

Tina was still at the clinic. "Did you find Grandad?"

"Yes. He's fine and so's Hector," said James. "They're both at the center."

"Thank goodness." Tina pointed to the whiteboard. "Mrs. Wicks brought in a guinea pig she found on the side of the road. I put it in the bathroom."

"Let's hope that's all," said James. "I'll take over here now."

"I'd better get back to Mum," said Tina. "I'll see you later, James. Bye, Stamp. Bye, Ace." She knelt and gave us both a really good rub around the ears. I had to give her another stamp of approval. As for Ace, she wagged her tail so fast I could hardly see it.

It was daylight when Doc came back from the center. "The fires are finally out," he said to James. "There's rain forecast for later today, too. That should make doubly sure we're out of danger."

"What happens now?" asked James.

"A lot of cleaning up and rebuilding," said Doc. "People whose houses and fences aren't damaged will probably take their animals back today or tomorrow, but I think some of the others will need to stay on."

"We can help out for a few more days," said James.

Doc grinned broadly. "I was hoping you'd say that."

So we did. The newspaper reporters

came around interviewing people and
did a story on James and how he'd come
to Jasper to find Daisy Ado's owner
and stayed on to help out. Then the
photographer took a picture. Of course,
Ace tried to eat her shoelace.

The day our picture was in the
newspaper, Daisy's owner, Al, came to get
her. He had bandages on his hands and

he was using crutches to walk. It turned out Daisy and Al didn't live in Jasper at all. Al had a house out in the bush. He'd been out fighting fires with the rest of the Rural Fire Brigade when the tree crashed on Daisy's aviary. He'd had an accident and had to go to the hospital. Daisy must have flown quite a long way!

When Al came into the cottage, Daisy spread her wings and screeched with delight. "Daisy Ado! Daisy Ado!" She hopped onto his shoulder and rubbed her beak on his chin.

Two days after that, James decided it was time for us to move on.

"So," said Tina to James as we were getting into the Fourby. "You didn't have to come into Jasper at all."

"No," said James. "It's been an adventure, though! Bye, Tina. Bye, Doc."

"Bye, James, bye, dogs," said Tina. "You never know . . . we might see you all again sometime."

Later that day, Dad and Mum Barnaby called James on the radio.

"What's all this about you fighting fires and saving birds, James?" asked Dad Barnaby. "Jeannie sent us a clipping from the paper. Over."

"It wasn't quite like that . . ." said James. "Over."

"It was a lovely photo of you and Stamp," said Mum Barnaby. "But who was the sweet little dog next to you in the picture? Over."

"Ah," said James. And he told them all about Ace.

A Word on Fire Safety for Pets

If you need to evacuate your house because of a fire, don't forget your pets. Have an evacuation plan for them. Always have them in a pet carrier or a harness. If your pet wears a collar, it is a good idea to have your name, address and phone number on the tag. An emergency pack for a dog might include vet records and contact information in a waterproof bag, food and bottled water. A familiar blanket or toy may help calm your pet if it has to go to a shelter.

Catch Stamp, Ace and
James in their first
Pup Patrol adventure!

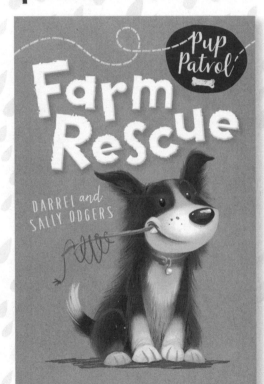

Farm Rescue
Available now!